Summer
Story

Jill Barklem

HarperCollins *Children's Books*

For David

For more information visit the Brambly Hedge website at:
www.bramblyhedge.com

First published in hardback in Great Britain by
HarperCollins Publishers Ltd in 1980
First published in paperback in 1995
This edition published by HarperCollins Children's Books in 2012

1 3 5 7 9 10 8 6 4 2

ISBN: 978-0-00-746153-0

HarperCollins Children's Books is a division of HarperCollins Publishers Ltd.

Text and illustrations copyright © Jill Barklem 1980

Visit our website at: www.harpercollins.co.uk

Printed and bound in China

Brambly Hedge

For many generations, families of mice have made their homes in the roots and trunks of the trees of Brambly Hedge. If you are ever lucky enough to be nearby, you may see a wisp of smoke from a small chimney or even a steep flight of stairs deep within the trunk of a tree.

Mrs Apple

The mice of Brambly Hedge lead busy lives. They make all their own food and during the fine weather, they collect herbs,

Mr Apple

fruits and nuts from the hedge and surrounding fields. They then prepare delicious jams, pickles and preserves that are kept safely in the Store Stump where Mr Apple is the Warden. Mr Apple's wife, Mrs Apple, is the very best of cooks and their home, Crabapple Cottage, is always filled with the aroma of cakes and freshly baked bread.

Although the mice work hard, they always have time for fun. They welcome the opportunity to meet and celebrate and their favourite place for a party is the Old Oak Palace. This is where Lord and Lady Woodmouse live with their young daughter Primrose.

Primrose

Lord & Lady Woodmouse

Primrose's best friend is Wilfred Toadflax who lives in the hornbeam tree at the end of the Hedge. Wilfred and his brother Teasel love to play tricks on their sisters Catkin and Clover.

These are just a few of the mice that live in the Hedge. Meet some of their friends and relatives in *Summer Story*.

Wilfred

It was a very hot summer.

Each day the sun rose high in the blue sky, and the fields shimmered in the heat.

The hedgerow was quiet. Many of the mice preferred to stay inside their shady cottages, trying to keep cool.

Out of doors, the best place to be was down by the stream. The mice gathered there in the afternoon, sat under the bank in the shade, and dangled their paws and tails in the clear water.

On the banks of the stream were the flour and dairy mills. The flow of the water turned the wheels which ground the flour and churned the butter for Brambly Hedge.

Poppy Eyebright looked after the Dairy Stump. She supervised the large vat into which milk, kindly given by some friendly cows, was poured and stored. The many kitchens, where cheeses were drained and shaped, smoked and wrapped, were also in her care.

Poppy was not fond of hot weather. Her pats of
butter began to melt unless they were wrapped in cool
dock leaves, and the pots of cream had to be hung in
the millpool to keep them fresh.

When her work was finished she would wander out
by the millwheel, enjoying the splashes of cool water.

The flour mill, further down the stream, was run by
the miller, Dusty Dogwood. Dogwood was his family
name, but he was called Dusty because
he was always covered from tail
to whiskers with flour dust.

He was a cheerful and friendly mouse, like his father,
his grandfather, and his great-grandfather, who had all
run the mill before him. He loved the fine weather and
strolled up and down the stream, chatting to the paddlers
and dabblers.

His walks took him past the Dairy, where he would
often see Poppy standing by the stream, looking very
pretty. As the long, hot days went by, Dusty used to
spend more and more time walking up to the Dairy,
and Poppy used to go out more and more often to the
mossy shadows of the millwheel…

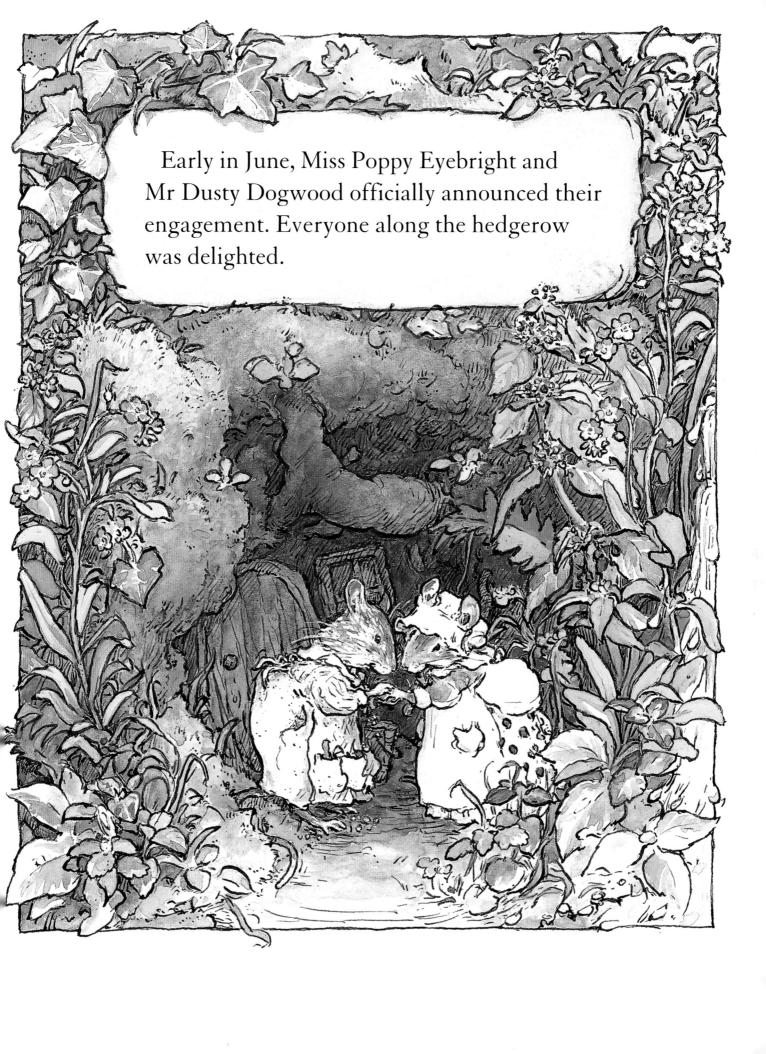

Early in June, Miss Poppy Eyebright and
Mr Dusty Dogwood officially announced their
engagement. Everyone along the hedgerow
was delighted.

Midsummer's Day was picked for the wedding and preparations were started at once. Poppy was so sure the weather would hold that they decided that the wedding should take place on the stream. It was the coolest place, and besides, it was very romantic.

Dusty found a large, flat piece of bark up in the woods, which a party of mice carried down to the water's edge. It was floated, with some difficulty, just under the mill weir, and tethered in midstream by plaited rush and nettle ropes.

Poppy prepared her trousseau. Every afternoon,
she sat in the shade of some tall kingcups embroidering
her wedding dress, which she hid as soon as she saw
anyone coming along the path.

The wedding day dawned at last. The sky was clear
and blue and it was hotter than ever. The kitchens
of Brambly Hedge were full of activity. Cool summer
foods were being made. There was cold watercress
soup, fresh dandelion salad, honey creams, syllabubs
and meringues.

The young mice had been up early to
gather huge baskets of wild strawberries.
   Basil selected some white wines,
primrose, meadowsweet and
elderflower, and hung them to
cool in the rushes. Basil was in
charge of all the cellars under the Store Stump. He was
a stout, good-natured mouse, with long white whiskers
and a sensitive nose for fine wine.

In her rooms above the Dairy, Poppy dressed carefully. She polished her whiskers and dabbed rosewater behind her ears. Her straw bonnet, which Lady Woodmouse had trimmed with flowers, hung from the bedpost, and her bridal posy lay waiting on the windowsill. She peeped at her reflection in the shiny wardrobe door, took a deep breath, and ran downstairs to join her bridesmaids.

Dusty kept his best suit in a basket under the stairs to protect it from the moths. He put it on and tucked a daisy in his buttonhole. "I'd better just check that barley I ground yesterday," he said to himself. He ran up the steps at such a pace that the whole mill seemed to shake. The wooden floor above him let down a cloud of dust, all over his new wedding suit.

"Bother it!" he said, sitting on a sack of corn and looking at his mottled jacket in dismay.

There was a thumping on the door below and his friend Conker called through the letterbox, "Dusty, are you ready? It's nearly time to go."

Dusty sighed and went morosely down the stairs.

As soon as Conker saw him, he began to giggle.

"Dusty by name, dusty by nature," he said, trying to remedy matters with his clean handkerchief.

The floury dust swirled and settled again on whiskers, tails, best clothes and buttonholes. The two mice looked at each other and started to laugh. They laughed so much that they had to sit down on a flour bag to recover.

The wedding was to take place at midday and Dusty and Conker arrived just in time. The guests were all in their finest clothes. Three young mice, dressed in smart blue suits, had been chosen as pages and were busily directing everyone to their places. Mrs Apple discreetly tried to dust down the groom and best man, but to little avail.

At last old Mrs Eyebright, Poppy's grandmother, spotted the bride and her little bridesmaids coming through the grass. The pages squeaked with excitement and got into place. Every head turned to watch the bride as she made her way through the buttercups and stepped on to the decorated raft.

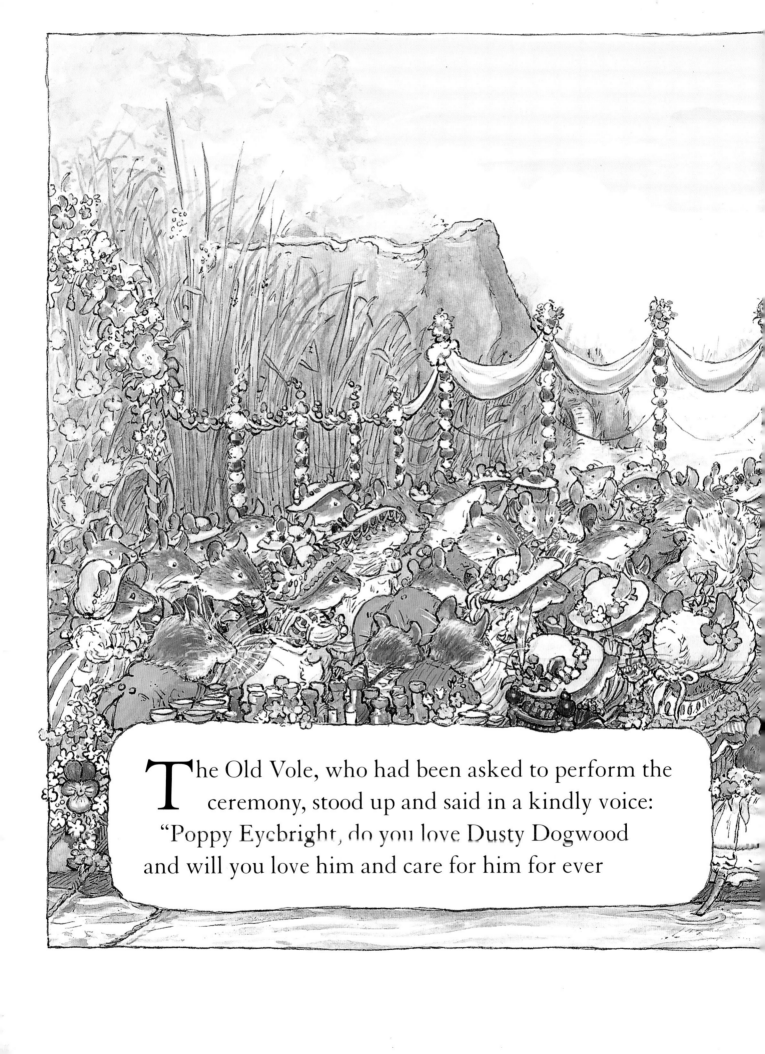

The Old Vole, who had been asked to perform the ceremony, stood up and said in a kindly voice: "Poppy Eyebright, do you love Dusty Dogwood and will you love him and care for him for ever and ever?" Poppy vowed that she would.

"Dusty Dogwood, do you love Poppy and will you love her and look after her for ever and ever?"

"I will," said Dusty. Mrs Apple blew her nose.

"Then in the name of the flowers and the fields, the stars in the sky, and the streams that flow down to the sea, and the mystery that breathes wonder into all these things, I pronounce you mouse and wife."

All the mice cheered as Dusty kissed his bride, and the bridesmaids threw baskets of petals over the happy couple. Mrs Apple wiped a tear from her eye and the dancing and feasting began.

First they danced, for no one could keep still, jigs, reels and quadrilles.

Mr Apple proposed a toast.

"To the bride and groom! May their tails grow long, and their eyes be bright, and all their squeaks be little ones."

The guests raised their glasses and then they danced again. The dancing was so vigorous that the raft bobbed up and down. Gradually the ropes holding the raft began to wear through.

One by one, the little ropes snapped, until finally the very last one gave way.

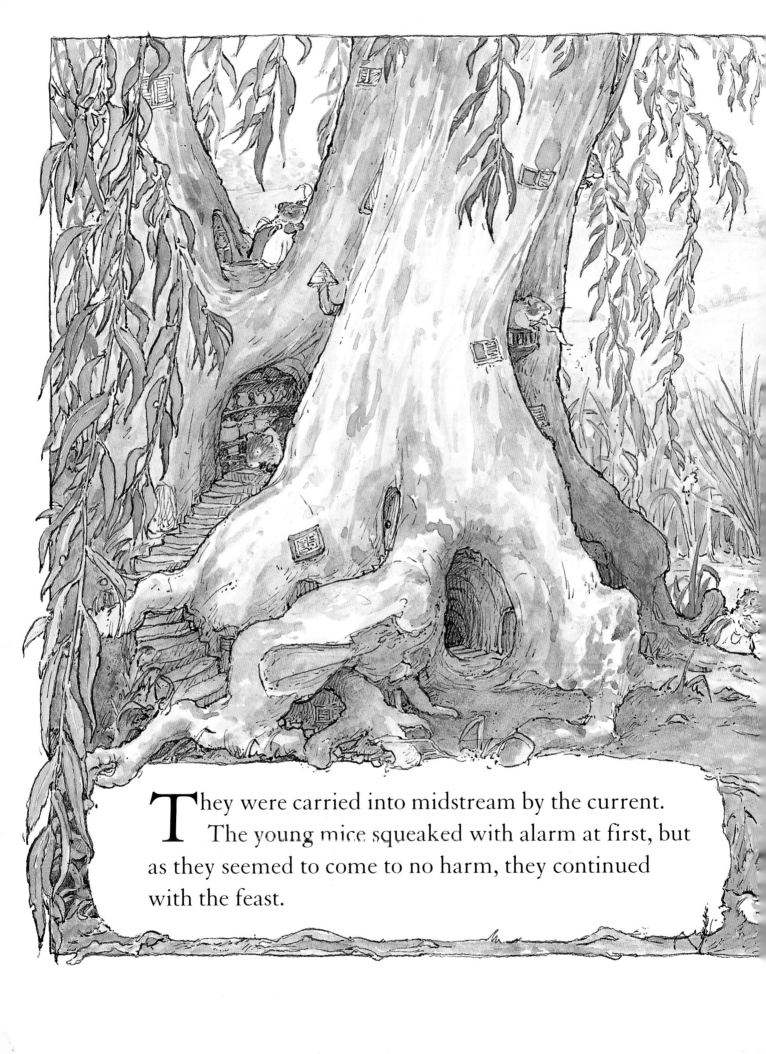

They were carried into midstream by the current.
The young mice squeaked with alarm at first, but
as they seemed to come to no harm, they continued
with the feast.

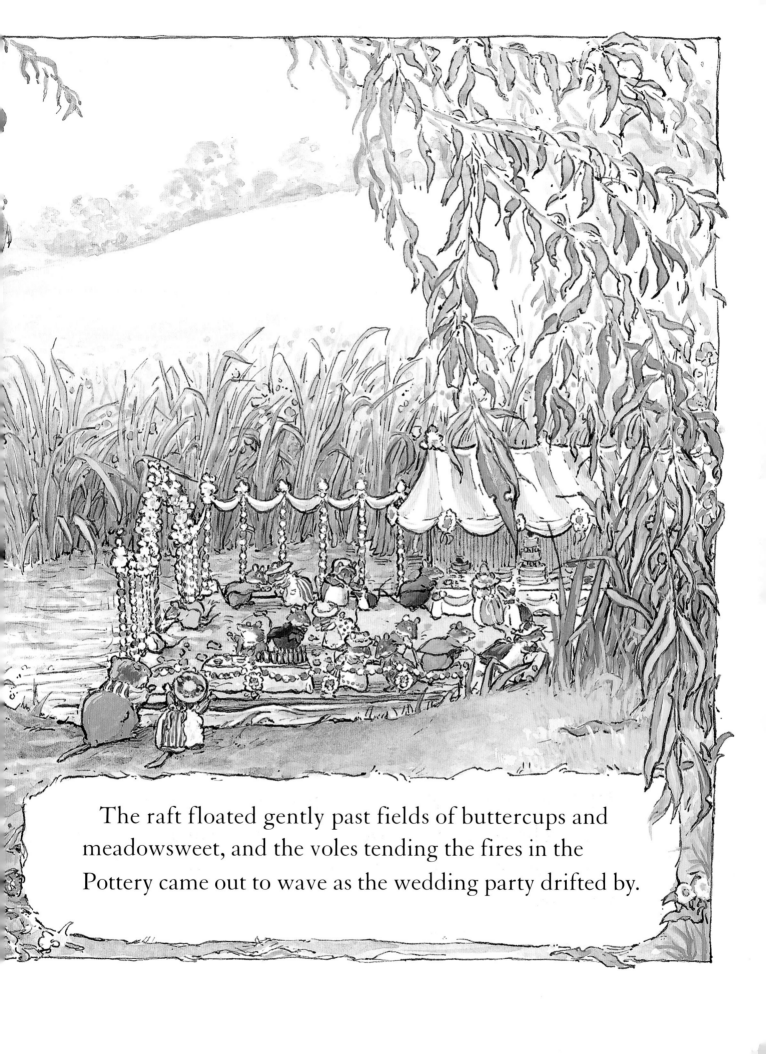

The raft floated gently past fields of buttercups and meadowsweet, and the voles tending the fires in the Pottery came out to wave as the wedding party drifted by.

Eventually, the raft was caught in a leafy clump of rushes and forget-me-nots. The ropes were made fast and the dancing began again.

At last the dusk came, golden and misty over the
fields. The blue sky slowly darkened and the mice
began to think about getting home. All the food was
finished up and the pots and pans hidden in the
rushes to be collected the next day.

They walked back through the fields in the evening
sun, looking very splendid in their wedding clothes.
The Old Vole was taken back to his hole first and the
rest of the mice gradually made their way home to
bed, exhausted but happy.

And what happened to Poppy and Dusty?
They slipped quietly away to the primrose woods. The primroses were over, but there, hidden amongst the long grass and ferns, wild roses and honeysuckle, was the cottage in which they had chosen to stay.

It was the perfect place for a honeymoon.